This book belongs to:

....

Published by the Penguin Group
Penguin Books Ltd, 80 Strand, London WC2R 0RL, England
Penguin Group (Australia) Ltd, 250 Camberwell Road, Camberwell, Victoria 3124,
Australia (a division of Pearson Australia Group Pty Ltd)
Individual titles first published by BBC Children's Character Books, 2008
This compilation edition first published by BBC Children's Character Books in 2009
This edition published by BBC Children's Character Books in 2010
10 9 8 7 6 5 4 3 2 1
**Based upon stories, songs and rhymes from In the Night Garden,
as authored and composed by Andrew Davenport.**

Text and design © BBC Children's Character Books, 2008
In the Night Garden characters and logo ™ & © Ragdoll Worldwide Limited 2007.
In the Night Garden is a trademark of Ragdoll Worldwide Limited.
Produced by Ragdoll.
Licensed by BBC Worldwide Ltd.
BBC Logo™ & © BBC 1996.
www.inthenightgarden.co.uk
ISBN: 978-1-40590-766-8
Printed in China

Story Treasury

8 favourite stories

Andrew Davenport

Contents

The night is black,
And the stars are bright,
And the sea is dark and deep,
But someone I know,
Is safe and snug,
And they're drifting off to sleep.

Round and round,
A little boat,
No bigger than your hand,
Out on the ocean,
Far away from land.

Take the little sail down,
Light the little light.
This is the way to the
Garden in the night...

Shall we go by **Ninky Nonk...**

or shall we go by **Pinky Ponk?**

What a funny noise!

Once upon a time in the Night Garden...

Makka Pakka came to play.

Makka Pakka,
Akka wakka,
Mikka makka moo!

Hum dum,
Agga pang,
Ing ang ooo!

Makka Pakka,
Appa yakka,
Ikka akka ooo!

Makka Pakka,
Akka wakka,
Mikka makka moo!

One day, Makka Pakka
was getting his Og-pog ready.

He packed his sponge,
his soap,
and his Uff-uff.

What else?

Makka Pakka's trumpet!

Makka Pakka loves
his trumpet.

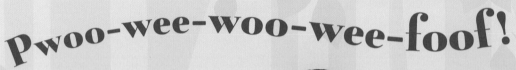

Pwoo-wee-woo-wee-foof!

What a funny
trumpet noise.

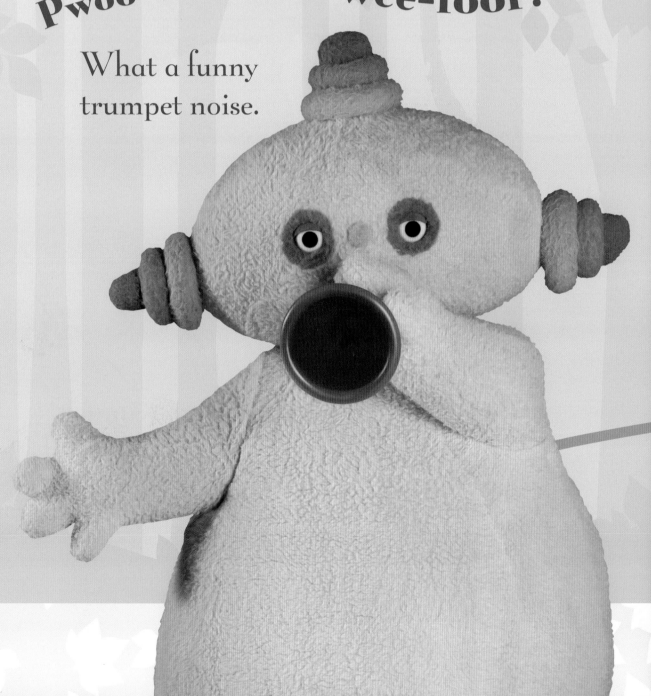

Pwoo-wee-woo-wee-foof!

What a funny
trumpet noise again!

Oh dear.
There is something wrong
with Makka Pakka's trumpet.

Upsy Daisy and Igglepiggle were out for a walk in the garden.

Pwoo-wee-woo-wee-foof!

What a funny noise!

Oooo-ooo!
Upsy Daisy and Igglepiggle
met Makka Pakka.

Pwoo-wee-woo-wee-foof!

What a funny trumpet noise,
Makka Pakka!
What are we going to do?

Pwoo-wee-woo-wee-foof!

Upsy Daisy, are you going to do a dance?

Makka Pakka, are you going to join in?

What fun!

26

Rattle-rattle-rattle!

Wait a minute.
What's that noise?

Rattle-rattle-rattle!

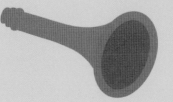

Something was rattling
inside Makka Pakka's trumpet.

Do you know what it was?

A very pretty stone.

What a funny thing!

Parp-parp!

That's a proper
trumpet sound,
Makka Pakka.

Makka Pakka gave
the pretty stone
to Upsy Daisy
as a present.

Makka Pakka's trumpet
was making a funny noise
because it had a stone in it.

Isn't that a pip?

Once upon a time
in the Night Garden,
there was a funny noise.

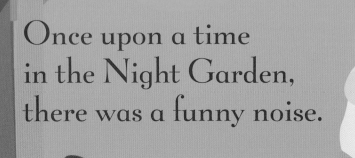

Pwoo-wee-woo-wee-foof!

What a funny noise,
coming from
Makka Pakka's trumpet.

Makka Pakka had a stone stuck in his trumpet.

Makka Pakka gave the stone to Upsy Daisy.

Thank you, Makka Pakka.

Too much
Pinky Ponk juice!

Once upon a time in the Night Garden...

The Tombliboos came to play.

Ombliboo Tombliboo,
    knock on the door.
Ombliboo Tombliboo,
    sit on the floor.
Ombliboo Tombliboo,
    here is my nose.
Ombliboo Tombliboo,
    that's how it goes!

One day the Tombliboos
were riding in the Pinky Ponk
with Upsy Daisy
and Igglepiggle.

Tombliboo Ooo drank up all
his Pinky Ponk juice.
Do you know what
Tombliboo Ooo did next?

42

Sluurrp!

That's not Tombliboo
Ooo's Pinky Ponk juice.

Sluurrp!

Neither is that!

Tombliboo Ooo drank everybody's
Pinky Ponk juice.

Wobble-grobble...

44

Grumble-burble-bluuurp!

Oh dear. Tombliboo Ooo has too much Pinky Ponk juice in his tummy.

Poor Tombliboo Ooo.

Wobble-grobble-grumble... burble-bluuurp!

Tombliboo Ooo went straight to bed.

Tombliboo Unn and Tombliboo Eee began to play a Tombliboo tune especially for Tombliboo Ooo.

Tiddly-plinky-plonky-onk!

Tombliboo Ooo listened.
And he began to feel better.

Tombliboo Ooo jumped out of bed
and ran all the way down
the Tombliboo stairs.

Tombliboo Ooo gave Tombliboo Unn
and Tombliboo Eee a big Tombliboo hug.

Look at that.
One, two, three happy Tombliboos.

Isn't that a pip?

Once upon a time
in the Night Garden,

Tombliboo Ooo
drank up all of
the Pinky Ponk juice.

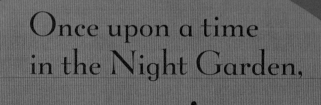

Sluurrp!

Sluurrp!

Wobble-grobble-grumble!
Poor Tombliboo Ooo.

Tombliboo music
will help!

Thank you Tombliboo Unn,
thank you Tombliboo Eee.

Upsy Daisy loves
the Ninky Nonk!

Once upon a time in the Night Garden...

Upsy Daisy came to play.

Upsy Daisy! Here I come,
I'm the only Upsy one!
I'm the only Daisy too,
Ipsy Upsy Daisy doo!

One day, Upsy Daisy decided to kiss
everything in the garden.
What a funny idea, Upsy Daisy!

Upsy Daisy doo!

First of all she kissed
her friend, Igglepiggle.

Then Upsy Daisy kissed a tree

Upsy Daisy doo!

a flower,

Upsy Daisy doo!

the Magical Gazebo,

Upsy Daisy doo!

and another tree.

What a lot of things
there are to kiss
in the garden,
Upsy Daisy.

Ting-ting!

Upsy Daisy decided to go by Ninky Nonk.

What a very clever way to kiss everything in the garden, Upsy Daisy.

Ting-ting!

The Ninky Nonk stopped.
Look at that.
What a lot of daisies!

Upsy Daisy doo!

Upsy Daisy gave every single daisy a big Upsy Daisy kiss.

Ting-ting!

The Ninky Nonk stopped again.
Who's here?

Makka Pakka!

Hello Makka Pakka.

Upsy Daisy doo!

Upsy Daisy gave Makka Pakka
a big Upsy Daisy kiss.
Makka Pakka was very pleased.

Ting-ting,
pinkle-tinkle,
onky-tonk,
whoooooomph!

Oh dear.
What a funny noise!

What was the matter
with the Ninky Nonk?
Do you know?

Has Upsy Daisy
remembered to give
the Ninky Nonk a kiss?

Upsy Daisy!

Upsy Daisy gave the Ninky Nonk
a great big Upsy Daisy kiss.

Upsy Daisy doo!

Ting-ting!

What a happy
Ninky Nonk.

Upsy Daisy!

The Ninky Nonk
wanted a kiss.

Isn't that a pip?

Once upon a time
in the Night Garden,

Upsy Daisy kissed a tree,
Igglepiggle, all the daisies
and Makka Pakka.

Upsy Daisy, you forgot
to kiss the Ninky Nonk!

Upsy Daisy doo!

What a happy Ninky Nonk.

Thank you,
Upsy Daisy.

Where is Igglepiggle's blanket?

Once upon a time in the Night Garden...

Igglepiggle came to play.

Yes, my name is Igglepiggle!
Iggle-piggle-wiggle-niggle-diggle!
Yes, my name is Igglepiggle!
Igglepiggle-niggle-wiggle-woo!

Igglepiggle has a favourite thing.
Do you know what it is?

It's Igglepiggle's blanket.

84

One day, Igglepiggle
lost his blanket.
Has anybody seen
Igglepiggle's blanket?

Tombliboo!

The Tombliboos hadn't seen
Igglepiggle's blanket.

Don't worry, Igglepiggle.
We'll find your blanket.

Brring-brring!

The trubliphone is ringing.

Who is calling on the trubliphone?

Mi-mi-mi-mi-mi-mi-mi!

Said a teeny tiny voice.

Igglepiggle didn't know
who it was.

Has anybody seen
Igglepiggle's blanket?

Upsy Daisy!

Upsy Daisy hadn't seen
Igglepiggle's blanket.

90

Don't worry, Igglepiggle.
We'll find your blanket.

Brring-brring!
The trubliphone
is ringing again.

Who is calling on the
trubliphone?

Mi-mi-mi!

Mi-mi-mi-mi-mi-mi-mi!

Mi-mi-mi-mi-mi!

Said lots of teeny tiny voices.

Igglepiggle still didn't know
who it was.

Has anybody seen
Igglepiggle's blanket?

Makka Pakka!

Makka Pakka hadn't seen
Igglepiggle's blanket.

Mi-mi-mi-mi-mi-mi-mi!

Who is that calling, Igglepiggle?

Look at that.
It's Igglepiggle's blanket!

Mi-mi-mi-mi-mi-mi-mi-mi-mi!

Said Igglepiggle's blanket.

Igglepiggle's blanket
doesn't usually say
Mi-mi-mi-mi-mi-mi-mi-mi-mi!

Igglepiggle picked up his blanket.
There was something underneath...

The teeny tiny Pontipines!
So that's who was calling on the trubliphone!

Igglepiggle's blanket was on top of
the Pontipine's house!

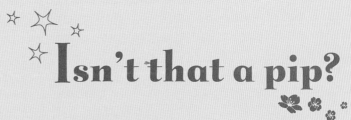

Isn't that a pip?

Once upon a time
in the Night Garden,
Igglepiggle lost his blanket.

Brrrring-brrrrrring!
The trubliphone rang.

Mi-mi-mi-mi-mi-mi-mi!

Who is calling on
the trubliphone?

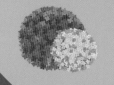

There is your blanket
Igglepiggle!

And there are
the Pontipines!

Thank you, Pontipines.

Where are the Pontipines?

Once upon a time in the Night Garden...

The Pontipines came to play.

The Pontipines are friends of mine,
Although they're only small -
And even when there's ten of them,
They're hardly there at all!

One day, the teeny tiny Pontipines went for a very long walk.

around the tree stump,

Through the log,

behind the flowerpots,

up a tree,

down again,

and in and out of the teeny tiny hole.

What a very long walk!

Over the bridge,

under the branch,

up and over Upsy Daisy's bed,

through the long grass.

What a very, very long walk.

The little Pontipine children were feeling tired.

Wait a minute, Mr and Mrs Pontipine.
Where are the children?

Mi-mi-mi-mi-mi!

said Mr Pontipine.

Mi-mi-mi-mi-mi!

said Mrs Pontipine.

Mrs Pontipine looked through her binoculars.

Do you know what she saw?

Look at that.

The teeny tiny
Pontipine children
were feeling so tired,
they had all
gone to sleep in
Upsy Daisy's bed.

Only Upsy Daisy
is allowed to
go to sleep in
Upsy Daisy's bed!

Upsy Daisy!
Upsy Daisy!

Who's here?

It's Upsy Daisy!

Wake up little
Pontipine children!
Upsy Daisy is coming back.

114

But the teeny tiny Pontipine
children were fast asleep.

Boing!

Upsy Daisy sat down on her bed.

Boing...

The teeny tiny Pontipine children all woke up.

Boing... boing... boing... boing!

Upsy Daisy bounced on her bed.

Boing... boing... boing... boing!

The teeny tiny Pontipine children bounced too.

And do you know what happened?

The teeny tiny Pontipine
children bounced right out
of Upsy Daisy's bed!

Up, and up, and up they went.

Miiiiiiiiiiiiiiiiiiiiiiiiiiii!

And down,
and down,
and down...

...into the little chimney of the teeny tiny Pontipine house.

The teeny tiny Pontipine children went

mi-mi-mi-mi-mi!

all the way home.

Isn't that a pip?

Once upon a time
in the Night Garden,

the teeny tiny
Pontipine children
went to sleep in
Upsy Daisy's bed.

Boing!

The teeny tiny Pontipine children bounced all the way home.

Thank you, Upsy Daisy.

Where is the Pinky Ponk going?

Once upon a time in the Night Garden...

The Pinky Ponk came to play.

Igglepiggle, iggle onk,
we're going to catch...

...the Pinky Ponk!

One day Igglepiggle, Upsy Daisy,
the Tombliboos and Makka Pakka
went for a ride on the Pinky Ponk.

Somebody else went too.

Mi-mi-mi!

Do you know who it was?

The teeny tiny Pontipines, of course!

Ponk! Ponk! Ponk!

Where is the Pinky Ponk going?

Over Upsy Daisy's bed...

over Makka Pakka's house...

over the Tombliboo bush...

Ponk! Ponk! Ponk!

Where is the Pinky Ponk going?

Up and up...
and up.

Higher and higher...
and higher.

Into the branches
of a very tall tree.

Ponk! Ponk! Ponk!

Where is the Pinky Ponk going?

Up and up...
and up and up,
went everybody
in the Pinky Ponk.

Higher and higher...
and higher and higher,
right to the very top
of the tree.

And do you know what they saw?

Look at that.
A special thing. That is the bud
of the Olly-bolly-dob-dob flower.

Very rare indeed.

And look – it's beginning to open!

One flower,

two flowers,

three flowers,

four!

More... and more... and more... and more!

The Olly-bolly-dob-dob flower!

The Pinky Ponk took us all that way, just in time to see the Olly-bolly-dob-dob flower.

Isn't that a pip?

Once upon a time
in the Night Garden,

the Pinky Ponk took everybody
to see a special thing.

The Olly-bolly-dob-dob flower.
Thank you, Pinky Ponk.

Igglepiggle lost!

Once upon a time in the Night Garden...

Igglepiggle came to play.

Yes, my name is Igglepiggle!
Iggle-piggle-wiggle-niggle-diggle!
Yes, my name is Igglepiggle!
Iggle-piggle-niggle-wiggle-woo!

One day, Igglepiggle went looking for his friends in the garden.

Upsy Daaaaaiisy!

Upsy Daisy was singing.

Clack-clack-clatter!

Makka Pakka was tidying his stones.

The Tombliboos were playing Tombliboo music.

Plink-plonk-bang!

What a lot of noisy noises, Igglepiggle!

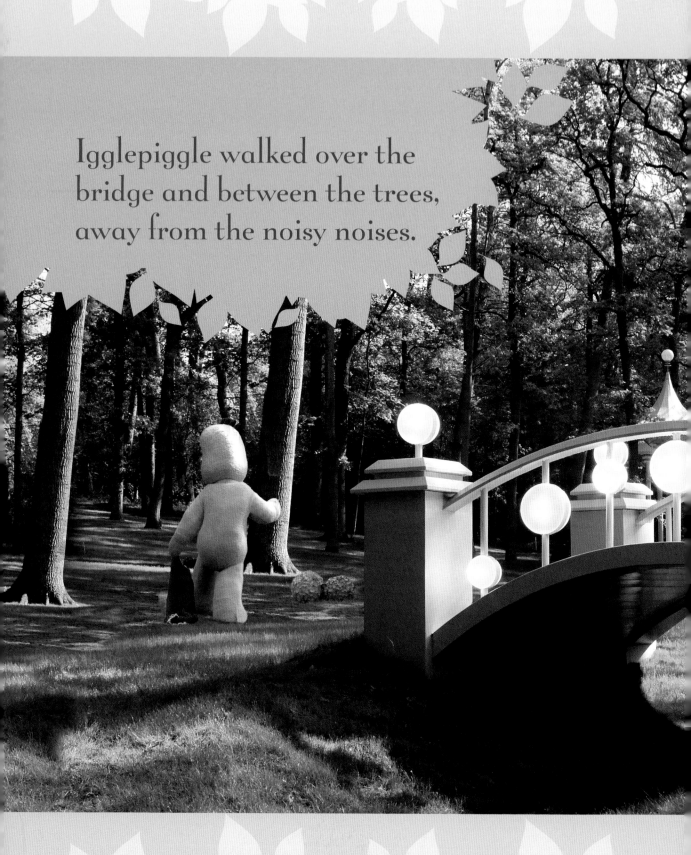

Igglepiggle walked over the bridge and between the trees, away from the noisy noises.

Igglepiggle found a quiet part of the garden.

That's better, Igglepiggle.
No noisy noises here.

Then it was time to go home.
Which way, Igglepiggle?

Oh dear.
Igglepiggle didn't know which way to go.
Igglepiggle was lost.

Mi-mi-mi-mi-mi!

Who's here?

Mrs Pontipine looked through her binoculars and saw Igglepiggle lost.

Mi-mi! she said.

Mr Pontipine picked up the trubliphone.

First he called Upsy Daisy.

Then he called Makka Pakka.

Then he called the Tombliboos.

Mi-mi-miiiiiii!

What was
Mr Pontipine
telling everybody?

Upsy Daaaaaaiiisy!

Make more
noise singing,
Upsy Daisy!

Clack-clack-clatter-clack!

Make more
noise tidying,
Makka Pakka!

Plink-plonk-bang-bang!

Make more noise playing music, Tombliboos!

Altogether, it was the noisiest noise ever heard in the garden.

What is that noisy noise, Igglepiggle?
Is it your friends?

Follow the noisy noises!

Igglepiggle followed the noisy noises,
between the trees and over the bridge.

Igglepiggle
found his friends.

Igglepiggle loves his noisy friends.
And everybody loves Igglepiggle.

Isn't that a pip?

Once upon a time in the Night Garden, Igglepiggle was lost.

The Pontipines called on the trubliphone.

Make more noisy noises
everybody!

Igglepiggle followed
the noisy noises
all the way home.

Igglepiggle loves
his noisy friends.

Tombliboo trousers on the Ninky Nonk!

Once upon a time in the Night Garden...

The Ninky Nonk came to play.

Igglepiggle, iggle onk,
we're going to catch...

...the Ninky Nonk!
Everybody loves the Ninky Nonk!

Here comes the Ninky Nonk.
All aboard the Ninky Nonk!

Tombliboo!

Makka Pakka!

Hello Tombliboos!
Hello Makka Pakka!

The Ninky Nonk went
all over the garden.

Up a tree,

upside down,

along a branch...

and down the tree again.

What a silly Ninky Nonk.

Tombliboo!

Hold on to your trousers, Tombliboos!

At last the Ninky Nonk stopped.

Bye-bye, Makka Pakka!
Bye-bye, Ninky Nonk!

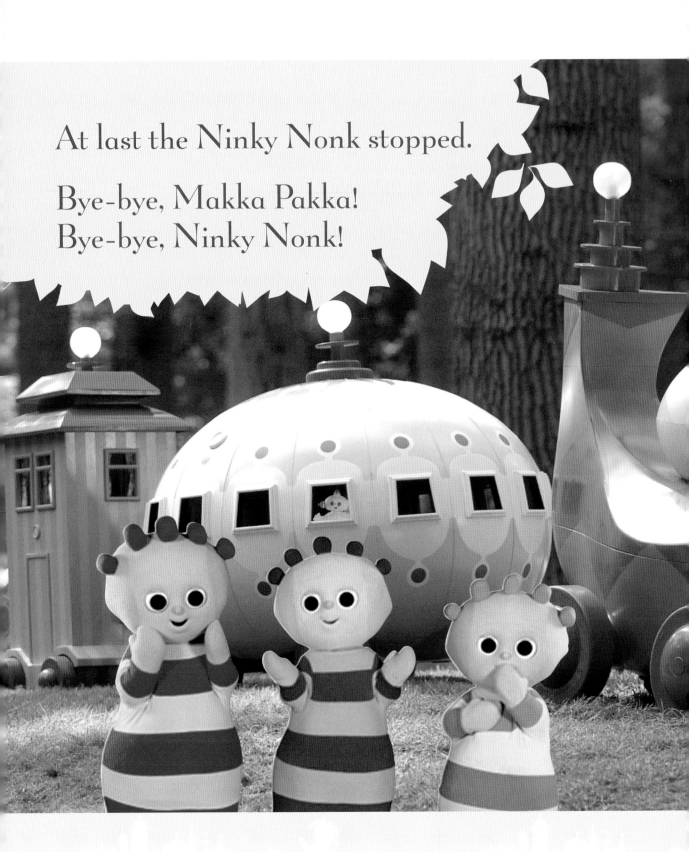

Wait a minute,
Tombliboos –
where are your
Tombliboo trousers?

The Tombliboos
had left their trousers
on the Ninky Nonk!

Catch the Ninky Nonk,
Tombliboos!

Tombliboo!

But the Tombliboos couldn't
catch the Ninky Nonk.
They had to go home without
their Tombliboo trousers.

Poor Tombliboos.

Tombliboo!

Who is getting off the Ninky Nonk?

It's Makka Pakka!

Makka Pakka!

Where is Makka Pakka
going?

What is Makka Pakka
carrying on his Og-pog?

Makka Pakka carried the Tombliboo trousers all the way back to the Tombliboo bush.

Makka Pakka!

Makka Pakka blew his trumpet.

Parp-parp!

The Tombliboos looked
out of the windows.

Tombliboo!

The Tombliboos were very pleased to see
Makka Pakka...

Makka Pakka!

Tombliboo!

and very happy to see their trousers.

One, two, three happy Tombliboos.

Tombliboo!

Thank you, Makka Pakka.

The Tombliboos love their
Tombliboo trousers.

Tombliboo!

The Tombliboos love
Makka Pakka.

Makka Pakka!

Makka Pakka loves
the Tombliboos...

and everybody loves
the Ninky Nonk.

Isn't that a pip?

Once upon a time
in the Night Garden,

the Tombliboos and Makka Pakka
went for a bouncy ride.

Oh dear, Tombliboos.
Where are your
Tombliboo trousers?

Makka Pakka brought the
Tombliboo trousers all the
way back to the Tombliboo
washing line.

Thank you, Makka Pakka.

Time to go to sleep
everybody.

Go to sleep,
Makka Pakka.

Go to sleep,
Upsy Daisy.

Go to sleep,
Tombliboos.

Go to sleep,
Pontipines.

Go to sleep,
Haahoos.

Go to sleep Ninky Nonk
and go to sleep, Pinky Ponk.

Wait a minute.
Somebody is not in bed!
Who's not in bed?
Igglepiggle is not in bed!

Don't worry, Igglepiggle...
it's time to go.